C901438010

LIBRARIES NI
WITHDRAWN FROM STOCK

Brainy
BORIS

D1390222

ORCHARD BOOKS
Carmelite House, 50 Victoria Embankment, London EC4Y 0DZ
Orchard Books Australia
Level 17/207 Kent Street, Sydney, NSW 2000

First published in 1998 under the title
BORIS THE BRAINIEST BABY by Orchard Books
This updated version published in 2015

ISBN: 978 1 40833 756 1

Text © Laurence Anholt 2015
Illustrations © Tony Ross 1998

The rights of Laurence Anholt to be identified as the author and Tony
Ross to be identified as the illustrator of this work have been asserted by
them in accordance with the Copyright, Designs and Patents Act, 1988.

A CIP catalogue record for this book is available
from the British Library.

1 3 5 7 9 10 8 6 4 2

Printed and bound by CPI Group (UK) Ltd, Croydon, CR0 4YY

The paper and board used in this book are made from wood
from responsible sources.

Orchard Books is an imprint of Hachette Children's Group and published by
the Watts Publishing Group Limited, an Hachette UK company.

www.hachette.co.uk

Brainy BORIS

Laurence Anholt

Illustrated by Tony Ross

ORCHARD

www.anholt.co.uk

Hee, hee, hello everyone!
My name is **Ruby** and I have the funniest family in the world.
In these books, I will introduce you to my **freaky family**.

You will meet people like…

Tiny Tina

Bendy

Ben

Poetic Polly

Mucky Micky

Brave Bruno

Hairy Harold

But this book is all about…my brainy brother, **BORIS**.

We are going to meet my brainy baby brother Boris, the brainiest baby ever born. I cannot tell you how brainy my brother is. He is just too brainy for words.

The minute Boris was born, he shook hands with the doctor and kissed his mother.
"Hello," he said. "I am Boris, the brainiest baby ever born."

All the nurses in the hospital came running. They had never seen a new baby dress himself.

Boris put on a tiny suit.

Boris put on a tiny bow tie.

My brother Boris took a tiny
umbrella and stepped outside.

My mum and dad said, "Boris,
you are too young to leave the
hospital."
"Yes," said all the doctors. "You
are only one hour old."

"Nonsense!" said Boris. "I am Boris, the brainiest baby ever born. I have many things to do. Please call a taxi."

When they arrived home, my mum
tried to give Boris a big cuddle and
a sloppy kiss.

But Boris didn't have time for
cuddles or sloppy kisses. He had to
get to school.

"Boris, you are too young to go to school," said my dad. "You are only one morning old."

"Nonsense!" said Boris. "I am Boris, the brainiest baby ever born. Here comes the school bus. Goodbye."

Boris liked it at school. The teacher
showed him a nice picture book.
"Look, Boris. Here is a woof-woof
and a quack-quack," she said.

"Nonsense!" said Boris. "That is not a woof-woof. And that is not a quack-quack. It is a dog and a duck. It is time you learned the proper words."

"This baby is too brainy," said the teacher. "This baby is too brainy to be at school."

So Boris went home. My dad went to tuck him into his cot. But Boris was on the telephone. "I'm finished with school," said Boris. "Now I'm trying to find a job."

"Boris, you are too young to get a job," said my mum and dad. "You are only one day old."

"Nonsense!" said Boris. "I am
Boris, the brainiest baby ever born.
My train leaves in the morning.
Goodnight."

The next day, Boris took a train to the city. He started work at a big office at the top of a high tower.

"Good morning, everybody," said Boris. "I am Boris, the brainiest baby ever born. Let's make money."

Boris liked it at the office. He had a
big desk and lots of telephones.

At lunchtime, my mum and dad came to change his nappy and give him a hug. But Boris was far too busy on the computer.

"Perhaps there will be time for a hug at the weekend," said Boris. "Please talk to my secretary."

The people at the office said, "This baby is too brainy to work in our office. He should be the boss of our company."

That evening, Boris came home
late. My mum and dad were
waiting up. They had bought him
a pink, fluffy bunny.

"I am too busy for bunnies,"
said Boris. "I am the boss of a
big company. I have to fly away
for an important meeting. The
plane leaves in one hour. I must
pack my bag."

"Boris, you are too young to be the boss of a big company," said my mum and dad. "You are only two days old."

"Nonsense!" said my brother, Boris. That night, he flew in a plane to another country. Boris liked going to other countries. He liked learning to speak new languages.

The Prime Minister of the country
came to see Boris, the brainiest
baby ever born.

"You are too brainy to be the boss of a big company," said the Prime Minister. "You should be a Prime Minister, like me."

"Yes!" shouted all the people.
"You should be a Prime Minister,
like him."

Then Boris flew back. He began to feel very tired. He wished he had his pink bunny.

At home, I had helped my mum paint some fluffy lambs on Boris's nursery wall.

"I expect you are ready for a nap and a cuddle now," said my dad.

Boris thought for a moment. He
thought it would be nice to have
a nap and a cuddle in the nursery
with the fluffy lambs on the wall.

But then Boris said, "No. I am
Boris, the brainiest baby ever born.
I am going to be Prime Minister.
I am going to go on television to
talk to everyone. The show starts in
ten minutes."

Lots of people came to the house.
There were bright lights and
television cameras and lots of noise.

Everybody was ready to start.
Everybody in the country was
sitting at home watching TV.
They wanted to see my brother
Boris, the brainiest baby ever born.
They wanted to see Boris, the
Prime Minister.

But Boris had gone. Nobody could
find him.
The people looked everywhere.
They ran all over our house with
their television cameras.

Boris was not on the telephone.

Boris was not at his computer.

Boris was not ready to talk on the television.
At last they found him. Boris was in the nursery with the fluffy lambs on the wall.

"Shhh!" said my mum.
"Shhh!" said my dad.
Boris was in his cot, cuddled up
with his pink bunny.

My brother Boris, the brainiest
baby ever born, was fast asleep.
After all, he was only four days old.

THE END

MY FREAKY FAMILY

COLLECT THEM ALL!

Also available as an ebook